Ngalculli
The Red Kangaroo

For
DICK ROUGHSEY O.B.E.
My colleague and friend
of many beautiful years

Angus&Robertson
An imprint of HarperCollins*Publishers,* Australia

First published in Australia by William Collins Pty Ltd in 1986
First published in Australia in paperback in 1988
This Angus & Robertson Bluegum paperback published in 1990
Reprinted in 1993, 1996
by HarperCollins*Publishers* Pty Limited
ACN 009 913 517
A member of the HarperCollins*Publishers* (Australia) Pty Limited Group

HarperCollins*Publishers*
25 Ryde Road, Pymble, Sydney, NSW 2073, Australia
31 View Road, Glenfield, Auckland 10, New Zealand
77-85 Fulham Palace Road, London W6 8JB, United Kingdom
Hazelton Lanes, 55 Avenue Road, Suite 2900, Toronto, Ontario M5R 3L2
and 1995 Markham Road, Scarborough, Ontario M1B 5M8, Canada
10 East 53rd Street, New York NY 10032, USA

National Library of Australia Cataloguing-in-Publication data:

Trezise, P. J. (Percy J.).
Ngalculli, the red kangaroo.
ISBN 0 207 17035 5.
[1.] Aborigines, Australian – Legends – Juvenile literature.
2. Red Kangaroo – Folklore – Juvenile literature.
I. Title.
398.2'45292

Typeset by Savage Type Pty Ltd, Brisbane
Printed in Hong Kong

9 8 7 6 5 4   96 97 98 99

Ngalculli

The Red Kangaroo

Percy Trezise

Angus&Robertson
An imprint of HarperCollins*Publishers*

In the beginning in Dreamtime, the Kangaroo people
had changed themselves into red kangaroos. They were
travelling together in a big mob down Cape York Peninsula.

An old man kangaroo led the way, followed by all the does and younger kangaroos. Ngalculli came along last, so he could watch over all the others in case there was any trouble. Red kangaroos always travel that way.

The Bird people were camped on the Dua River.
They had not yet changed into birds, as it was in a time
before the trouble with the Flying Fox people.

They were dancing in a big corroboree before going out
to hunt kangaroos and fish, and to gather yams and fruit.
The men had spears, and the women yamma sticks for digging.

The young men and boys were sent out to find the
kangaroos, and then drive them to where the older men
were hiding with spears ready. Milkee, the Frog-mouthed
owl, had made his own spear, but Goodbulboon, the
Butcher-bird, told little Milkee to go with the young men.

"No Grandfather," Milkee said, "I want to spear a kangaroo myself."

Goodbulboon said, "You are too little to spear a kangaroo, you must go and drive the kangaroos to us." But Milkee kept pleading until the men agreed to let him stay, but to keep hidden well back behind them.

The spearmen spread out in a line from the river, hiding behind
trees, antbeds and bushes, to await the arrival of the kangaroo mob
being driven toward them by the young men and boys.

Milkee waited until all the hunters were busy watching for the
coming kangaroos, then he crept up closer and hid behind an antbed.
He wanted to spear a big kangaroo to show his grandfather
he was growing into a strong and brave hunter.

The kangaroos came in a big mob, travelling fast and kicking up
a lot of dust, with Ngalculli booming along at the back.
The Birdmen started spearing kangaroos, which were soon
falling over everywhere.

A spear just missed Ngalculli and he jumped on the spearman, knocking him over. Milkee threw his little spear at the mighty Ngalculli, hitting him in the flank.

It was only a small, light spear. Ngalculli pulled
it out of his flank and smelt it, looked about, and sniffed
the air to see who had speared him.

Ngalculli saw Milkee, he grabbed him, placed him on his back, and hopped away. Milkee hung on tightly, he was very frightened. All the other spearmen were so busy they did not notice what had happened to Milkee.

When the Birdmen noticed that Milkee was missing they
looked about for his tracks, but could not find any.
Goodbulboon sent two Swallow men, the Warrenjoogu-joogu
brothers, to look for his tracks. They flew off,
each making a big semi-circle.

They met again without seeing any trace of Milkee.
The Swallows flew in another big circle and met again.

"No, he is not there. He must be going another way,
we will have to travel far to the south and wait for him."

Ngalculli bounded along with Milkee clinging to his neck in terror.
Ngalculli had seen his son killed by one of the spearmen
and he wanted to make Milkee his son to replace him.

He made mighty leaps across gorges, rivers and creeks as they
travelled south, following on the tracks of the kangaroos
who had escaped the spearmen. Each evening he stopped
and made a flat place to camp.

Ngalculli travelled south for many days, following the tracks
of the fleeing red kangaroos. Each day the tracks were getting
fresher and Milkee was getting more used to his terrifying ride.

One evening, while travelling along through a red sandstone gorge, they came on the rest of the kangaroos where they had stopped to camp. None of them liked the idea of Ngalculli trying to make Milkee his son. They did not like the Bird people with their spears.

The Swallow brothers were camped at the mouth of
the red gorge, because they knew everyone travelling
south would have to pass through it.

Early one morning they felt the ground shaking and soon
saw the red kangaroos. They waited until Ngalculli went past,
last as usual, and saw Milkee on his back.

The Swallows flew high in the air, then swooped down,
each catching hold of one of Milkee's arms, and flew off with him.
They carried him far away so Ngalculli would not be able
to find him again.

They landed on a high hill among grey granite boulders
and said, "You are now Milkee the owl. You stand up tall with your
head up and eyes closed and no one will be able to see you.
You will look like a grey rock." The Swallow brothers flew away.

The red kangaroos had none of Milkee's tracks to follow
so they spread out and searched for him. Ngalculli urged
them to travel far and wide to find his son Milkee.

The Swallow brothers flew about, leading the kangaroos
in the wrong direction. Ngalculli hopped sadly around
looking for his lost son.

One night, Ngalculli woke up and heard someone calling
in the still night air, "Milkee, Milkee, Milkee."

"That is my son calling," said Ngalculli. "In the morning
I will go to the top of that hill and find him."

At dawn Ngalculli went to the top of the hill. He saw
Milkee standing there and said, "You have turned to stone,
my son. I will lie here beside you and also turn to stone.
This will be our Dreaming Place."

The Swallow brothers took the Bird people to see Milkee.
They saw the form in stone of Ngalculli lying beside him.
Goodbulboon said, "That is good. Now the Bird people and
Kangaroos will be friends. We will never kill each other again."

Ngalculli and Milkee remain side by side in their
Dreaming Place on the high hill in Cape York. It is called
Lighthouse Mountain, because Milkee, standing tall,
looks like a lighthouse.